To Ron,

Best Wishes—

David
Williams

Sept. 28, 1991

WALKING
TO THE
CREEK

by David Williams
Illustrated by Thomas B. Allen

ALFRED A. KNOPF
New York

THIS IS A BORZOI BOOK
PUBLISHED BY ALFRED A. KNOPF, INC.

Text copyright © 1990 by David Williams
Illustrations copyright © 1990 by Thomas B. Allen
All rights reserved under International and Pan-American Copyright
Conventions. Published in the United States by Alfred A. Knopf, Inc.,
New York, and simultaneously in Canada by Random House of Canada
Limited, Toronto. Distributed by Random House, Inc., New York.

Manufactured in Singapore
Book design by Paolo Pepe

2 4 6 8 0 9 7 5 3 1

Library of Congress Cataloging-in-Publication Data
Williams, David, 1953–   . Walking to the creek. Summary: A walk to
the creek behind the grandparents' farm is an occasion for exploring the
wonder and special beauty of nature. [1. Nature—Fiction] I. Allen, Thomas
B., ill. II. Title. PZ7.W655925Wal 1990 [E] 88-6763
ISBN 0-394-80598-4 ISBN 0-394-90598-9 (lib. bdg.)

To Daniel and Kelly
—D.W.

To my brother Jimmy
—T.B.A.

Our grandparents' farm is very old. Inside, the house smells of bread baking and apple pie. On the walls are pictures of us when we were little, and Mom and Dad holding us before we could crawl. My brother and I have been coming to visit the farm since we were babies. Everything sounds and looks different from the city; something's always going on.

Grandpa has two dogs, Teddi Sue and Sam. They're the great-great-grandkids of the ones that lived here with Mom. They follow us wherever we go, snooping, sniffing, stirring up rabbits, cats, sometimes even a skunk.

The barn is a big red wall against the sky. Behind it, the pigs wallow, eyes tiny as beads. "Pigs even *sound* muddy," we tell Grandpa, who says, "They're the cleanest animals on the farm and 'bout as smart as dogs." Teddi Sue and Sam would be insulted.

The goat out back we call Gramps, though his real name's Pierre Goatee. He kind of resembles Grandpa, with his white beard, and he's the orneriest animal on the farm. We don't call him Gramps when Grandpa's around, only Pierre Goatee.

The creek is about a half mile from the farm, by Mr. Brum's field. "Want to look at some fish?" I ask my brother. "You bet," he says, so we just start walking. Teddi Sue and Sam follow us, of course, and today they're chasing butterflies. There are hundreds of them. They look like scraps of colored paper someone threw out of a car.

The garden has been taken over by tomatoes. Sometimes I think they could populate the whole earth, but we eat them, so they can't. They're best topped with cottage cheese and pepper, or Grandma boils them down to sauce and stacks them in the cupboard in her big glass jars.

Zucchini are like dark green boats with hundreds of passengers inside. Bell peppers are fat and bulgy. We imagine them ringing all night long, disturbing the potatoes, who are asleep and getting fat below the ground.

Sometimes Grandma says, "Be careful, don't fall in the water" when we go walking to the creek, which is what she told Mom when she was growing up. Grandpa just says, "Have fun while you still can." Grandpa thinks he's too old to go with us, but I see him watching us as we get smaller and smaller, until finally we seem like part of the road.

Now the way is along chalk-white gravel. It's a high road we're on, but the corn is even higher. On the other side an army of soybeans is crouched low with broadleaf arms. The dogs run back and forth between the rows, like spies warning everyone we are near.

A pickup passes. We make way, holding Teddi Sue and Sam by their collars. Barn swallows swell overhead with their tail feathers pointed, forming perfect Vs. Pretty soon they're dive-bombing us, protecting nests we can't see. "Try shooing them!" I yell to my brother, who is just standing there with his hands over his eyes. Finally we have to run for it.

We're so out of breath, we don't realize we've gotten down to the creek. Then I see that it's different. Past the bridge it's the way it's always been: crooked, with the current moving slow as it twists around rocks. But on this side a fence goes through still water, and green oozes up, insects dancing on top. Everything has been bulldozed, and all the trees on the bank cut down. "It's like there's been a war," my brother says, squinting. The crooked side is full of life.

I climb on some old tree stumps, and my brother follows. There's a big oak lying nearby, and I start counting the rings on its stump. "Each year a new ring grows," I remember Grandpa telling me once when he was cutting logs. I touch the good years and the bad years, but my brother is only interested in finding minnows.

The cows pack the fencerow along the creek, their black hooves plodding the muddy line. They have shovel heads and eyes as large as yo-yos. They see us and stare. The pale moon rises over their heads, but they decide not to jump.

We walk on the trail near the water's edge. "This was the home of the Potawatomi, of the Sauk and Fox," Grandpa has told us. He says there are still arrowheads in the soil, and axe heads that are rare as whooping cranes. I keep my eyes close to the earth, looking for signs.

Teddi Sue and Sam go running ahead, and pretty soon we lose them. I whistle, but only Sam comes back. We keep walking. I'm calling, "*Teddi* S-U-U-U-E!" but she seems to be nowhere.

Past the bridge the mud bank is full of prints: raccoon, opossum, skunk, rabbit, and deer. We see a place where more trees have been cut down and garbage has been dumped and burned. Piles of old tires lie scattered about. We look inside one and find a brown nest with black feathers in the center.

Tall grass sways along the bank. We cup our hands around our mouths, screaming, *"Here, Teddi!"* I imagine her stuck in a brier patch after trying to catch some Br'er Rabbit who's just sitting on his hind legs, laughing, thinking she sure was dumb.

A muskrat sticks his head up and swims by. Sam sees him, howls, and jumps into the water. When Sam comes out, he doesn't seem too happy. He shakes himself on me until so much water's coming off his back, it's like he's soaked up half the creek. My brother laughs, but then Sam gets friendly with him, so I have my turn.

The sun is buoyed on corn tassels, on its way down. The sky is turning purple and red as we go on, calling for you know who.

As we leave the creek the water sound is the only thing. But then we hear a whisper sneaking up on us in the corn. Sam rushes after it, barking. It keeps getting louder, and we jump back, trying to see what could be making such a racket.

Teddi Sue leaps from the field, wagging her tail. She's a mess of burrs, which we'll have to pull out of her hair later. She runs to us, prancing up and down, and we hold her. We ask where she's been, but she doesn't tell us anything.

Heading back to the farm together, we feel like we've walked all the way to China. The sun has set, and we go toward the dark of the trees. Our grandparents' house is a single yellow light on the hill.

Back at the farm they're waiting for us. There is food to eat
from the garden. Grandpa tells us stories. Grandma *tsk tsks*
when Grandpa's tales get too tall. The dogs are outside, eating
from their dishes, then they're whining to get in.

As the Big Dipper rises, Grandma and Grandpa finally say good night. We try to go to sleep, but we hear crickets, bull-frogs, an owl, so we sneak Teddi Sue and Sam into the house and let them stay beneath our beds.

When we dream, we dream of our parents. We dream of our grandparents, of the farm and the creek. We dream of all the things that are living in this world.